蔡榮勇 著
Poems by Tsai Jung-yung

陳義超 譯
Translated by Chen Yi-chao

# 過
# 再
# 一
# 年

## One
## more year

蔡榮勇漢英雙語詩集
Mandarin-English

台灣詩叢 • Taiwan Poetry Series 14

# 【總序】詩推台灣意象

叢書策劃／李魁賢

　　進入二十一世紀，台灣詩人更積極走向國際，個人竭盡所能，在詩人朋友熱烈參與支持下，策畫出席過印度、蒙古、古巴、智利、緬甸、孟加拉、尼加拉瓜、馬其頓、秘魯、突尼西亞、越南、希臘、羅馬尼亞、墨西哥等國舉辦的國際詩歌節，並編輯《台灣心聲》等多種詩選在各國發行，使台灣詩人心聲透過作品傳佈國際間。

　　多年來進行國際詩交流活動最困擾的問題，莫如臨時編輯帶往國外交流的選集，大都應急處理，不但時間緊迫，且選用作品難免會有不週。因此，興起策畫【台灣詩叢】雙語詩系的念頭。若台灣詩人平常就有雙語詩集出版，隨時可以應用，詩作交流與詩人交誼雙管齊下，更具實際成效，對台灣詩的國際交流活動，當更加順利。

　　以【台灣】為名，著眼點當然有鑑於台灣文學在國際間名目不彰，台灣詩人能夠有機會在國際努力開拓空間，非為個人建立知名度，而是為推展台灣意象的整體事功，期待開創台灣文學的長久景象，才能奠定寶貴的歷史意義，台灣文學終必在世界文壇上佔有地位。

　　實際經驗也明顯印證，台灣詩人參與國際詩交流活動，很受重視，帶出去的詩選集也深受歡迎，從近年外國詩人和出版社與本人合作編譯台灣詩選，甚至主動翻譯本人詩集在各國文學雜誌或詩刊發表，進而出版外譯詩集的情況，大為增多，即可充分證明。

　　承蒙秀威資訊科技公司一本支援詩集出版初衷，慨然接受【台灣詩叢】列入編輯計畫，對台灣詩的國際交流，提供推進力量，希望能有更多各種不同外語的雙語詩集出版，形成進軍國際的集結基地。

# 紀念我的爸爸——悼譯者陳義超先生
# In memory of my father
## － the dedicated translator Chen Yi-Chao

陳燕欣Victoria Chen

## 煮咖啡

　　雖然爸爸已經去世一年多了，我們仍然常常想起他日日坐在客廳沙發上翻譯文稿的身影。小時候有記憶開始，爸爸日日必定進行他的翻譯工作。慣常見到他逐字在稿紙上用鋼筆寫下文句，再用不同色的簽字筆反覆修改，成了我童年以至長大後很重要的回憶。有時他會黎明即起，以便獲得幾個小時能在出門上課前多一些工作時間。此時他會用一只摩卡壺煮上一杯濃縮咖啡（我起床後仍能聞到），一邊逐字寫下翻譯稿。我至今仍記得那只舊咖啡壺和他慣常購買咖啡豆的老咖啡店。爸爸平日最喜歡喝茶和咖啡。猶記2019年春天爸爸發病前不久，我們購得一支手動磨豆機，他非常喜愛，常常在上午翻譯休息之際磨豆煮上一小杯咖啡，坐在餐桌前慢慢喝完。爸爸翻譯時，桌前必要擺上好幾部字典，有時還要進書房查詢更大更厚重的辭海。自幼時起，我便知道翻譯是爸爸生命中不可或缺的一部分。退休後，他將大部分的時間心力放在翻譯最喜愛的幾部作品，時常晨起游泳後便坐在客廳的桌前開啟一天的工作。至今，咖啡構成了我對他回憶中很重要的一部分，我也總記得他煮咖啡後留下咖啡粉漬放置於花盆土壤的習慣。

## 斟酌打磨

翻譯者之於字句，如同音樂家與樂器的反覆磨合，或畫家常年試煉油彩的濃淡。幼時我常見到爸爸對一句英詩字斟句酌，將一個句子反反覆覆推敲，在稿紙上整齊寫下一遍遍不同的版本，如同他最喜歡的巴洛克音樂，盤旋在相似的旋律中進行音階微調，微微改變主旋律的樂句。至今想起爸爸的日常作息，總是浮現書籍、文稿，和他最喜愛的巴哈大提琴無伴奏組曲。

## 游泳

　　晨起去泳池是爸爸的另一個終身嗜好。他總是致力於做每日的第一批泳者，年年如是，即便寒冷的冬日亦不改變。游泳後他會立刻回家，洗好泳衣後在餐廳坐下，簡單早餐後開始一天的翻譯工作。長年游泳如翻譯，都需要刻苦、毅力，以及深度的熱情。有時我們覺得爸爸的生活乏味，日後方才明白：簡單規律的生活才是他心之所向。我想他會告訴我們，翻譯和游泳的日常就如巴洛克音樂，平淡但有味。

## 無伴奏大提琴

　　爸爸享受孤獨，喜歡有充分的時間獨自工作。雖然他同時是一位深受學生愛戴和懷念的高中老師。退休後他屏除了大部分交際，致力於翻譯幾部最喜愛的作品，許多想和老師聯絡的學生常被他婉拒，直到爸爸去世後我們才聽聞學生們對他的深深懷念。如同他最喜愛的巴哈無伴奏組曲，爸爸的退休生活雖然缺乏人群簇擁，我們仍能在他的譯作中，感受到他享受到沉緬於字詞文句中深深的樂趣。

## 後記

　　2019年夏天，爸爸因右臉疼痛，意外檢查出鼻咽癌，直到同年十二月，病情忽然急轉直下。爸爸生命中最後幾個月暫停了工作，但各式字典仍擱在几上，直至他最後入院。直到今日，見到爸爸的書籍和字典，就想起他日常的作息和慣常談話。爸爸的葬禮上，一個個未曾謀面的學生和老友傾訴老師當年對文學、古典音樂、和電影的熱愛，如何改變了自己對人生的看法和方向。我們明白了爸爸不是真的逝去，只是以另一種方式活在許多愛他的人的心中。僅以此文紀念爸爸，以及他一生對文字的熱愛。

女兒燕欣2021年3月18日寫於台中

## Brewing coffee

　　It has been a year since my father's passing. Sometimes when I wake up in the morning walking past the living room, I swear I can still see him sitting on the sofa working on some translation project he has on hand.

　　As far back as I can remember in my childhood, father was always translating some literature. You always find him has the subject book in front of him along with several dictionaries and a thesaurus. A draft with versions of translation for each word that he writes with different colors of pen. Yes, there is no computer nor googling, the pain and the inconvenience from the old world is only fitting, respectable way for serious translation that he's working on.

Somehow I knew since I was a young child that translation is my father's true love, true career in the sense of giving him the greatest joy of accomplishment. During weekdays, he always gets up before dawn, so he can squeeze a couple hours to work on his project before work. As his morning ritual, he would also brew himself a cup of espresso before sitting down, as if this is the proper way to start a serious endeavor. On weekends when he gets to work on translation for a longer duration of time, he would slowly walk from his work area to the kitchen during break, grind the coffee bean and pour the hot water gently and intently, as if it's as serious as his translation work. After he retired from teaching, he spent most of his free time translating his favorite books, and it all started with that cup of coffee in the morning.

To date, I still remember vividly that old stained coffee mug and the hand grinder that he loves. And of course that freshly brewed coffee smell that still lingers in the house when I woke up.

## Brewing the words

My father respects translation. Every word, every sentence. The choice of each word, how one fits into the next word and the sentence, the paragraph, the chapter and the whole book. It's like a musician with notes and instruments, a painter with his shades and colors. Like Baroque music, the repeating of the chord but each turn it comes around with a slight tweak of the ornaments and contrasts. For each page of the book, I remember seeing a stack of drafts with different versions of the translation, handwritten in different ink colors, and hours of deep thoughts holding them down on the desk, like a paper weight. He respects the work, so he brews his choice words, like making a good cup of coffee.

## Swimming

Morning swim is another life long hobby of his. He always tries to be the first in the pool, everyday, be it sunny, cloudy, rainy or in the bitterness of the winter cold. Just like translation work, every morning swimmer requires passion and persistence. I remember being critical of my father's way of life as boring when I was young. After his passing when I was in remembrance, and having a chance to look at his life as a whole, I now realize a life of simplicity and form is his pursuit. To my critique, I imaging he would say " a life long of devotion to translation and morning swim is just like Baroque music, it's predictable yet enjoyable."

## Bach Unaccompanied Cello Suite No.1

My father does not mind social solitary, out of his desire of time to work on translation projects. Even though he was a highly popular english teacher, well loved by his students of the high school he teaches. After his retirement, he pretty much shunned all social gathering requests from his former students and colleagues. I only learned his popularity only after his passing, from the students and colleagues who came to pay respects at the funeral.

One of his favorite music is Bach's Unaccompanied Cello Suite No.1. Even though it's not grand like a symphony piece, with a singular cello, you can still hear the deeply buried, constrained passion.

## Epilogue

In the summer of 2019, my father went to the doctor due to the complaint of pain on his right cheek. Upon further testing, he was diagnosed with nasopharyngeal cancer. He received treatments but the disease took a turn for the worse in December of the same year. He was checked into the hospital as an inpatient for the last few months of his life and not able to continue his translation work as he would like.

In his funeral, many former students and colleagues who I have never met or heard of from my father showed up unexpectedly. They talked about how he has touched their lives by sharing his passion for literature, classical music and movies. I realized then my father did not leave us behind, he merely lived in our memory in another way. In another realm where he still sits in front of the desk, with books and dictionaries spread out and writing draft translations in different colored ink pens.

In memory of my father, who faithfully devoted his life to his passions.

By daughter, Victoria Chen,

written in our family home in Taichung, Taiwan.

March 18, 2021

# 目次

# 淡水詩歌節手札

坐在遊覽車上
眼睛刷過的街道
影像追逐瞬間的掉落

山對海說
感謝，你的遼闊
海對山說，你真挺

高爾夫球場
一隻白鷺鷥
寫了一首小詩

我從飯店的窗口探頭
觀音山也探出頭來
兩座高樓，不解風情

站在河岸看日落
夕陽，看得見
思念的心情

# 山櫻

山櫻，露出
紅色的微笑

# 友情

老友相見，這般甜蜜
時間有了香味
風喝到了，友情

# 微笑

細縫的水泥道
一株迷你野草
露出五瓣的黃微笑
膽怯的，告訴自己
春天，真的來了

# 蒲公英

朝陽擦拭著露珠
蒲公英的花瓣　黃色的花瓣
露出極限的笑容

# 日日春

春天來了
日日春的種籽
趕緊蹦進去

小孫女驚叫一聲
好美麗的一朵紅花

# 吉他

吉他裡面
一定住著一位神
演奏者
是他最忠實的信徒

# 人生的光彩

趕緊推開家單調，牆似的大門
請你來淡水，尋找快樂的鑰匙

追尋
紅毛城，異邦人的歷史印記

傾聽
馬偕教堂，馬偕牧師牧道的話語

登入
淡水老街，品嚐小吃、人文氣息

追憶
淡水漁人碼頭，繁榮的國際貿易

坐下
跟夕陽傾訴人生的美麗

# 上網

七嘴八舌
一句話
擠不出來
愛　停在半空中
上網

# 黃金風鈴木

親愛的泥土
請接納我們的任性

讓我們躺在您的懷抱裡
撒嬌一下

# 蔦蘿

紅色的星星
陽光下　熱情四溢
夜　暗不下來

# 七里香

行人說，好香喲
身體傾斜，聞一聞
泥土的根，好孤單

# 夕陽

燃燒的雲朵
為了煮熟
黑夜的晚餐

# 春的摺疊

每一片綠葉子
都是春的摺疊

石頭是這樣儲存
季節

# 忍不住

逃過寒天的浩劫
有一棵忍不住
睜開兩片新葉
同伴都還閉著眼睛
等待春天的美麗

# 春天說

請不要問我　為什麼
會開出紅紅又紅紅的花朵
去問大家　為什麼
喜愛紅紅又紅紅的花朵

# 黃扇鳶尾花

一根根的黃蠟燭
等待陽光來點火
是為誰慶生

風偷偷的說
為，今天

# 夕陽之二

夕陽
寫了一首小詩

海要讀一個晚上
藉著月光

## 玫瑰花

似開未開
有故事
耳朵想聽

似開未開
有神祕
眼睛想偷窺

# 香蕉

他們找尋
溫暖的家
急得，臉
都變黃了

# 樹

我站在這裡
就是一種風景
就是一首詩歌

鳥會來唱歌
風會來跳舞
陽光會來問候

# 白頭翁

我，孤單嗎
不，孤枝
比我還孤單呀

# 波斯菊

相信世界
就是一株波斯菊
努力追求開花的夢想

# 矮牽牛

陽台上
一群小美女
紅的白的黃的…

她們不知說了什麼八卦
眼睛，不禁多看了一眼。

## 禮物

使君子把紅花
當禮物
送給大樓
分享
大樓的笑容

# 陽光

陽光
也會口渴

杯子說

# 楓葉


哀愁的
楓葉

曾經綠過

# 遺忘的盆栽

枯乾的樹葉

樹根躲在花盆裡哭泣

陽光伸出愛之光

撫慰

盆子擦乾樹根的眼淚

像蝸牛換殼

轉換心情

等待新植物的來到

# 再過一年

再過一年
就可以退休了

拿著空袋子
要裝些什麼回家

打開回憶的保險箱
一年一次的考績證明

未來的人生
沒有教室也沒有學生

上班的　道　路
要自己尋找

再過一年
對過去的自己說一聲
再見

# 溪頭早晨的空氣

溪頭早晨的空氣
包圍我的身體
好像騎腳踏車
前進時輪子快樂的歌聲
溪頭早晨的空氣
好像削掉梨子皮
咬著　果肉
那般的甜味

離開溪頭
想到　小時候
媽媽抱我在懷中
聞到的那種芳香

# 吐新芽

阿爸阿母
跟植物是好朋友
用水跟他們談心

修剪枝葉時
植物光禿禿的抗議
過了幾天
伸出頭來道歉

阿爸阿母，笑嘻嘻的說
吐新芽了！
吐新芽了！

# 之間

畫與畫家
之間
建築自己的存在

收藏家與畫家
之間
建築觀賞的存在

畫廊與畫家
之間
建築了買賣的存在

之間
畫家無線的
天空

# 攝影

看不見的風景
傷悲　寂寞　心情　獨白……
眼睛　離家出走

看得見的風景
呼喚內心的風景
眼睛　思念家鄉

跟一根小草　對談
有時是自己的　寂寞
有時是自己的　傷悲

跟一棵大樹　對談
有時是自己的　心情
有時是自己的　獨白

跟一棟房子　對談
問自己要往何處去
問自己的家在何處

打開鏡頭　喃喃自語
喀嚓一聲　躍出鄉愁
救贖自己　內心的風景

# 開花

開花
是自我實現

是社會的貢獻
也是經濟行為

蝴蝶和蜜蜂
不再飢餓了

## 感謝組曲

秋風　謝謝你
你吹起了涼風
安慰了煩悶的心
盼望你也能吹走
我內心的苦悶

太陽　謝謝你
你趕走了黑夜
讓我的眼睛
看到了　黃脈刺桐的綠
看到了　掌葉蘋婆的綠

今天　謝謝你
讓我散步走路
讓我看見風景
謝謝你　拜託你
讓小貓安靜的睡覺

玫瑰花　謝謝你
你燦爛的笑容
安慰了憂鬱的心靈
安慰了死神的陰影
安慰了昨天的擔憂

玫瑰花　謝謝你
安慰了傷痛的心
跟隨蜜蜂鑽進你的心房
或許會見到女兒
甜美的笑容

阿母　謝謝你
讓我上學讀書
讓我喜歡閱讀
讓我喜歡寫作
讓我能夠孝順父母

仙人掌　謝謝你
讓我知道
不要用拳頭對抗陽光
留下小數點的細刺
告訴大家陽光長這個樣子

茶杯　謝謝你
每天讓我舒適的喝水
你自己從來都不渴
你不會口渴嗎
讓我感到不好意思

窗戶　謝謝你
讓我的眼睛
可以跟陽光聊天
讓我的心靈跟天空談心
讓我的身體感受到季節

草坪　謝謝你
讓我的眼睛和心靈
舒適地躺下來
你只寫一個　綠
我讀到許多　美

榕樹　謝謝你
讓我一片葉子
一片葉子的剪
從來都不生氣
馬上長出嫩葉

桌子　謝謝你
讓我們一家人
快樂的吃飯
愉快的喝茶
你從不抱怨

椅子　謝謝你
讓我坐下來讀書
讓我坐下來思考
讓我坐下來寫字
讓我坐下來祈禱

收音機　謝謝你
讓我的耳朵愉快
讓我的心靈愉悅
讓我的情緒開花
讓時間有節奏感

筆　謝謝你
讓我可以寫出
心中的喜怒哀樂
讓我可以寫出
夢中夢到的事情

字典　謝謝你
滿肚子的學問
一點也不吝嗇
讓我可以隨時翻閱
告訴我不懂的字義

秋葵　謝謝你
早晨睜開黑眼睛
對我露出微笑
憂愁的心靈
不再漆黑

時間　謝謝你
讓我感覺歲月
讓我感覺回憶
讓我感覺期待
讓我期待明天

# 夕陽之三

夕陽，是時間
在畫圓圈
畫一個句號的圓圈

黑夜裡
時間，仍然繼續
忙碌的寫作

# 後記

　　2020年2月5日早上到綠十七公園打太極拳，沒有見到陳老師過來打拳，心頭有點兒納悶。打拳結束後，往前向曾老師邀請到寒舍喝茶，曾老師告知1月11日癌細胞轉移無法搶救往生，好像被一支木棒驟然撞到心頭。陳老師幫我翻譯的短詩歌在心頭，上週方才找個時間稍加整理準備出版，發現篇數有點少，正想請他再多譯幾首。陳老師待人非常客氣，曾經到府拜訪幾次，客廳擺滿英美文學書籍，天天不是閱讀英美英文小說或是翻譯小說。竟日我想哭，哭不出來，眼淚直接攻入心頭。

# 作者簡介

　　蔡榮勇，1955年出生於台灣彰化縣北斗鎮，台中師專畢業。現為笠詩社社務兼編輯委員、台灣現代詩人協會理事、世界詩人組織（PPDM）會員。曾出版詩集《生命的美學》、《洗衣婦》及合集多種。2009年曾赴蒙古參加台蒙詩歌交流，2014年分別參加在古巴及智利舉行的國際詩歌節。

# 譯者簡介

　　譯者陳義超（Y.C. Chen，1950-2020），臺灣師大英語系畢
業。曾多次獲得梁實秋文學譯詩譯文獎。譯有《海的禮物》、
《我們的人》、《地糧》、《追憶非洲》。

再過一年
**One more year**

One more year

# Tamsui poetry festival notes

Sitting in a tour bus,

One scanned the streets

On which images dropped one following another instantly.


The mountain says to the sea,

「 Thanks, you are so vast. 」

The sea says to the mountain,

「 You are so erect. 」


In the golf course

A white egret

Has composed a cute poem.


Out of the window of the hotel I stretched my head

And Mt.Guanyin was stretching out its head too.

The two high buildings did not catch each other's

loving implications at all.

I stood on the river-bank, watching the sunset.

The setting sun could see

My reminiscent frame of mind.

# Mountain Cherries

Mountain cherries wear
Red smiles.

# Friendship

So sweet is a gathering of old friends.

Time smells fragrant and

The wind tastes friendship.

# A Smile

From a narrow

crack of a cement way

A tiny wild plant

Reveals its five-petal yellow smile

And timidly says to itself,

"The spring is really coming now."

# Dandelions

While the morning sunshine is wiping dewdrops,

Dandelion petals, Yellow ones,

Show their infinite smiles.

# Periwinkles

The spring is coming.

The seeds of periwinkles

Are jumping into it hurriedly.

My little granddaughter cries in surprise,

"How beautiful a red flower!"

# The Guitar

Inside the guitar

Surely lives a god.

The player

Is the most loyal follower of his.

# Splendors of Life

Push hurriedly out the wall-like dull home door ,and
Please come to Tamsui to seek the key of happiness,

To visit
Fort Santo Domingo, the remaining historical relic of
aliens,

To listen to
Church Mackay, an echo of the preaches of
Minister Mackay,

To step into
The ancient Tamsui streets to taste snacks and
an atmosphere of humanism,

To reminisce
The flourishing international trade on the Tamsui Fishmen's Quay, and

To sit down

To talk to the setting sun about the beauty of life.

# Logging onto the Internet

Everyone was saying at the same time.

One word was

Hard being uttered.

Love stopped halfway in the air

Logging onto the Internet.

# Golden Trumpet-tree

Dear Dirt

Please tolerate our obstinacy.

Let us lie on your arms

And have our pettish way for a while.

# The Star Glory

Red stars

Radiate passionately in the sun.

Night has difficulty falling down.

# Common Jasmin Orange

"How fragrant you are!" A pedestrian said,

Leaning over to smell flowers,

While the roots in the dirt felt very very lonely.

# The Setting Sun

Burning clouds
Are planning to cook well
The dinner for the night.

# Folding Spring

Every green leave
Is spring in folding.

Likewise a stone saves
Seasons.

# Couldn't Help It

Surviving the catastrophe of chilly days,

One of the trees could not help

Opening two new leaves,

While all its fellow trees still closed their eyes

Waiting for the beauty of spring.

# Spring Says

Please don't ask me　　why
I produce flowers so red red red and red.
Go ask everybody　　why
They love flowers so red red red and red.

# Yellow Walking Irises

One and another and another yellow candles

Awaiting the sun to light

For celebrating SOMEBODY's birthday

Wind says secretly

It's for TODAY.

# The Setting Sun II

The setting sun
Has written a cute poem.

The sea spends a whole night reading it
In the moonlight.

# Roses

Between budding and blooming
The roses seem to have stories
That ears are keen to listen to.

Between budding and blooming
The roses seem to have mysteries
That eyes are keen to peep .

# Bananas

They are searching for

A warm home

So anxiously that their faces

Are turning yellow.

# A Tree

Standing here

I am a sort of scenery

And a poem.


Birds will come here to sing.

Winds will come here to dance.

Sunshine will come here to greet.

# Light-vented Bulbul

Am I lonely?

No. A single twig

Is lonelier than I.

# A Cosmos

Believe me, the world

Is just a cosmos

Sparing no efforts to pursue its dream of blooming.

# Petunia

On the porch

A group of little beauties

In colors of red, white, yellow...

They seem to be gossiping something.

Eyes could not help but take one more glimpses at them.

# A Gift

Rangoon Creepers offer their flowers

As a gift

To the building

And share

Big smiles from the building.

# Sunshine

Sunshine
Feels thirsty too.

Says the cup.

# Maple Leaves

Sad and depressed
Maple Leaves

Have seen their own green good days.

# Forgotten Bonsai

Leaves are withering

While tree roots are hiding in the pot weeping.

The sunshine is stretching its light of love

To pat and comfort them

And the pot is wiping the tears of the roots, wanting

To change its own frame of mind and to wait for

The arrival of a new plant

Just like a snail's changing its shell.

# One more year

One more year
I am due to retire

Taking some empty bags
I want to pack things home

Then open the safe of my memory
Many an annual service grade certificate are there

For the life ahead
Neither classrooms nor students are awaiting me

For the way to daily work
I'll have to search anew

One more year

I'll say good-by to

The past of my own

# The Morning Air at Xi-tou

The morning air at Xi-tou
Around my body
Is like joyful songs of running wheels
When riding a bike
The morning air at Xi-tou
Is like biting a
Peeled pear
Tasting that sweet

Departing Xi-tou
I thought about Mom's hugging
In my childhood
Smelling that fragrant

# New Buds Are Coming out

Dad and Mom

Are good friends with plants

Watering them is their private chat with them

When pruning them

Bare plants were protesting gloomily

A few days later

Fresh buds lifted their heads to make an apology

Dad and Mom smilingly said

New buds are coming out!

New buds are coming out!

# Between

Between
Paintings and the painter
Establish his own existence

Between
Collectors and the painter
Bring appreciation into existence

Between
Galleries and the painter
Buying and selling comes into existence

The painter's limitless sky
Exists in
"Between"

# Photography

When the scenery is invisible

There remain sadness, loneliness, moods, monologue, ... ...

And stray eyes

When the scenery is visible

Images catch the inner scenes

And remembering eyes

When dialoguing with a blade of grass

You talk sometimes with your own loneliness

And sometimes with your own sadness

When dialoguing with a big tree

You talk sometimes with your own moods

And sometimes that is tour own monologue

When dialoguing with a house

You ask yourself where to go

And where your home is


Murmuring images

Snap to rescue

Your own scenery

# Flowering

Flowering

Is self-realization

Also social contribution

And economic behavior too

Butterflies and bees

Are not hungry any longer

# The Suite of Thanks

Thanks! The Autumn Wind

You blow cool

To console people in vexation

I expect you to blow away too

The distress and boredom in my heart


Thank! The Sun,

You chase away dark nights

And let my eyes

See the green of Erythrina Variegata 'Parcelli'

And the green of Hazel Sterculia


Thanks! Today

You let me take a stroll

You let me see the scenery

Thanks! I beg of you

To let my cat sleep quietly

再過一年
One more year

Thanks! The Rose

Your glorious smiles

Console melancholy minds

Relieve the shadow of Death

And relieve yesterday's worries


The Rose, thanks

For consoling my mournful heart

If I follow a bee to get into your ovary

I may see my daughter's

Sweet smiles


Thanks! Mom

You let me go to school

You let me enjoy reading

You let me enjoy writing

You let me fulfill my filial duty to you

Thanks! The Cactus

You let me know

Not to clench fists against the sun

Just leaving few fine needles

To tell everybody how the sun look like


Thanks! The Cup

You let me drink water comfortably

But you yourself never drink

Aren't you thirsty?

You make me feel a little uneasy


Thanks! The Window

You let my eyes

Chat with the sun

You let my mind have a tete-a-tete with the sky

You let my body feel the seasons

再過一年 ..............
One more year

Thanks! The Lawn
You let my eyes and mind
Lie down comfortably
You write just a stretch of green
And I read so much beauty

Thanks! The Banyan Tree
You let me prune your leaves
One by one
And never get angry
But sprout in no time

Thanks! The Table
You let all my family
Have meals happily
And drink tea joyfully
You never complain

The Chair, Thanks

For letting me sit on you to read

Letting me sit on you to think

Letting me sit on you to write

And letting me sit on you to pray


The Radio, thanks

For letting my eyes delight

Letting my mind feel happy

Letting my emotions flower

And letting time be rhythmical


The Pen, thanks

For letting me write down

The joy, anger, sorrow and delight in my heart

And letting me write down

Things in my dreams

Thank!, The Dictionary

You are not stingy at all

With all your broad knowledge

And let me consult you at any time

Telling me what I don't understand


Thank!, the Okra

You open dark eyes in the morning

To show smiles to me

And my melancholy mind

Is not pitch-black any longer


Time, thanks

For letting me feel age

Letting me feel remembrance

Letting me feel expectation

And letting me expect tomorrow

# The Setting Sun III

The setting sun seems that the time
draw circles
Draw a circle of a full stop

In the dark
Time keeps busy
busy writing

## About the Poet

Tsai Jung-Yung was born in Beidou, Changhua County, Taiwan in 1955. After graduating from Taichung Teachers' College, He went to Mongolia on the poetry exchange between Taiwan and Mongolia in 2009. He attended *International Poetry Festivals* respectively in Cuba and Chile in 2014.He is currently an editing member of *Li Poetry Group,* a director in *Taiwan Modern Poets' Association,* and a member of *PPDM.*

# About the Translator

    The translator Chen Yi-Chao (1950-2020), winner of Liang Shih-Chiu Literary Award (Translation Contest in Poetry and Prose), has translated "Gift from the Sea", "Nostromo", "Fruits of the Earth", "Out of Africa" into Chinese.

# CONTENTS

再過一年

**One more year**

語言文學類　PG2564　台灣詩叢14

# 再過一年 One more year
## ——蔡榮勇漢英雙語詩集

作　　　者／蔡榮勇（Tsai Jung-yung）
譯　　　者／陳義超（Chen Yi-chao）
叢書策劃／李魁賢（Lee Kuei-shien）
責任編輯／姚芳慈
圖文排版／周妤靜
封面設計／蔡瑋筠

發 行 人／宋政坤
法律顧問／毛國樑　律師
出版發行／秀威資訊科技股份有限公司
　　　　　114台北市內湖區瑞光路76巷65號1樓
　　　　　電話：+886-2-2796-3638　傳真：+886-2-2796-1377
　　　　　http://www.showwe.com.tw
劃撥帳號／19563868　戶名：秀威資訊科技股份有限公司
　　　　　讀者服務信箱：service@showwe.com.tw
展售門市／國家書店（松江門市）
　　　　　104台北市中山區松江路209號1樓
　　　　　電話：+886-2-2518-0207　傳真：+886-2-2518-0778
網路訂購／秀威網路書店：https://store.showwe.tw
　　　　　國家網路書店：https://www.govbooks.com.tw

2021年5月　BOD一版
定價：220元
版權所有　翻印必究
本書如有缺頁、破損或裝訂錯誤，請寄回更換

國家圖書館出版品預行編目

再過一年 One more year：蔡榮勇漢英雙語詩集
/ 蔡榮勇著；陳義超譯. -- 一版. -- 臺北市 :秀
威資訊科技股份有限公司, 2021.05
　　面；　公分. -- (語言文學類；PG2564) (台
灣詩叢；14)
　　BOD版
　　中英對照
　　ISBN 978-986-326-896-3(平裝)

863.51                                110004373

# 讀 者 回 函 卡

感謝您購買本書，為提升服務品質，請填妥以下資料，將讀者回函卡直接寄回或傳真本公司，收到您的寶貴意見後，我們會收藏記錄及檢討，謝謝！
如您需要了解本公司最新出版書目、購書優惠或企劃活動，歡迎您上網查詢或下載相關資料：http:// www.showwe.com.tw

您購買的書名：＿＿＿＿＿＿＿＿＿＿＿＿＿＿＿＿＿＿＿＿＿＿＿＿＿

出生日期：＿＿＿＿＿年＿＿＿＿＿月＿＿＿＿＿日

學歷：□高中 (含) 以下　　□大專　　□研究所 (含) 以上

職業：□製造業　□金融業　□資訊業　□軍警　□傳播業　□自由業
　　　□服務業　□公務員　□教職　　□學生　□家管　□其它＿＿＿

購書地點：□網路書店　□實體書店　□書展　□郵購　□贈閱　□其他

您從何得知本書的消息？

　□網路書店　□實體書店　□網路搜尋　□電子報　□書訊　□雜誌
　□傳播媒體　□親友推薦　□網站推薦　□部落格　□其他＿＿＿＿＿

您對本書的評價：（請填代號　1.非常滿意　2.滿意　3.尚可　4.再改進）
　封面設計＿＿＿　版面編排＿＿＿　內容＿＿＿　文／譯筆＿＿＿　價格＿＿＿

讀完書後您覺得：

　□很有收穫　□有收穫　□收穫不多　□沒收穫

對我們的建議：＿＿＿＿＿＿＿＿＿＿＿＿＿＿＿＿＿＿＿＿＿＿＿＿

＿＿＿＿＿＿＿＿＿＿＿＿＿＿＿＿＿＿＿＿＿＿＿＿＿＿＿＿＿＿＿＿

＿＿＿＿＿＿＿＿＿＿＿＿＿＿＿＿＿＿＿＿＿＿＿＿＿＿＿＿＿＿＿＿

＿＿＿＿＿＿＿＿＿＿＿＿＿＿＿＿＿＿＿＿＿＿＿＿＿＿＿＿＿＿＿＿

11466

台北市內湖區瑞光路 76 巷 65 號 1 樓

**秀威資訊科技股份有限公司**　　　收

BOD 數位出版事業部

..............................................................................

（請沿線對折寄回，謝謝！）

姓　　名：＿＿＿＿＿＿＿＿＿　年齡：＿＿＿＿　性別：□女　□男

郵遞區號：□□□□□

地　　址：＿＿＿＿＿＿＿＿＿＿＿＿＿＿＿＿＿＿＿＿＿

聯絡電話：(日) ＿＿＿＿＿＿＿＿＿　(夜) ＿＿＿＿＿＿＿＿＿

E-mail：＿＿＿＿＿＿＿＿＿＿＿＿＿＿＿＿＿＿＿＿＿